The God Game

Suzanne Bradbeer

SAMUEL FRENCH

FOUNDED 1830

SAMUELFRENCH.COM
SAMUELFRENCH-LONDON.CO.UK

THE GOD GAME received its world premiere on January 17, 2014 in a coproduction between Gulfshore Playhouse (Kristen Coury, Producing Artistic Director), and Capital Repertory Theatre (Maggie Mancinelli-Cahill, Producing Artistic Director). The Production Stage Manager was Kate Haggerty and the Assistant Stage Manager was Tory Sheppard. The set design was by Ken Goldstein; the costume design was by Jennifer Bronsted; original music and sound design was by Brad Berridge (also the Voice of the Reporter); the Props Mistress was Jennifer Murray; and the lighting design was by Deborah Constantine. The production was directed by Kristen Coury with the following cast:

TOM . . . . Laurence Lau

LISA . . . . Yvonne Perry

MATT . . . . Jeffrey Binder

The Gulfshore/CapRep production continued at Capital Repertory Theatre, opening May 6, 2014. The Production Stage Manager was Ashley Dumas, the Assistant Stage Manager was Kierian Cochran; the Props Mistress was Chelsea Leach; and the Voice of the Reporter was Joe Phillips.

THE GOD GAME was then produced in September 2014 at Stark Naked Theatre Company in Houston, Texas (Kim Tobin-Lehl & Philip Lehl, Co-Executive Directors). The Production Stage Manager was Rachel Dooley-Harris. The set design was by Jodi Bobrovsky, lighting by Andrew Vance, costumes by LA Clevenson, props by Tina Montgomery, and sound by Yezminne Zepeda. The Voice of the Reporter was Kevin Dean. The production was directed by Jennifer Dean with the following cast:

TOM . . . . Justin Doran

LISA . . . . Kim Tobin-Lehl

MATT . . . . Philip Lehl

Next in 2014 was the Hudson Stage Company production; Denise Bessette, Dan Foster, and Olivia Sklar, Executive Producers. The Production Stage Manager was Jason Weixelman and the Assistant Stage Manager was Jessie Jardon. The set design was by David L. Arsenault, lighting by Andrew Gmoser, costumes by Charlotte Palmer-Lane, props by Jeanette Mieses, and sound by William Neal. The Voice of the Reporter was Jane Beller. The production was directed by Giovanna Sardelli with the following cast:

TOM . . . . Robert Farrior

LISA . . . . Yvonne Perry

MATT . . . . Michael Frederic

The God Game was developed at the Lark Play Development Center, the Actors Studio P/D Workshop, the Playwrights Unit of the Ensemble Studio Theatre, and at the Dorset Theatre Festival/ Theresa Rebeck Writer's Colony.

It was chosen for the inaugural NEXT ACT! New Play Summit at Capital Repertory Theatre, and was a winner of the Ashland New Plays Festival.

CHARACTERS

TOM – 40s. The Junior Senator from Virginia.
LISA – 40s. His wife.
MATT – 40s. Their best friend.

TIME

A Saturday in August. The present.

SETTING

Richmond, Virginia. Tom's office at his home in the Fan District. A comfortable, welcoming room.

ACT ONE

(Lights up on **TOM** *at his laptop.* **LISA** *enters.)*

LISA. There you are, Senator.

TOM. *(not looking up)* I've got one more email.

(She watches a moment as he types.)

I promised to send over my notes on the Blake Commission.

(She watches a moment longer. He is completely preoccupied.)

It'll only take a few minutes… *(still typing)* to tell them they used a lot of fancy words…

*(***LISA*** slips off one of her shoes.)*

And wasted a whole lot of taxpayer money…

(She drops the shoe to the floor.)

On an eighteen month Commission…

(She slips off the other shoe.)

Just to tell us what we already know.

(She drops the second shoe to the floor.)

(looking up for the first time)

What are you doing?

(She is removing another article of clothing.)

LISA. I'm removing my clothes.

TOM. Bad idea.

LISA. Don't worry, we're alone.

TOM. That's not the point.

LISA. I beg to differ. That's exactly the point.

(She continues undressing.)

TOM. Lisa.

LISA. Are you worried your wife will find out?

TOM. No, but –

LISA. Then I don't see a problem.

TOM. The problem is that I'm a very important man, with very, very important things that I do.

LISA. And that's so very, very fascinating but you need to stop talking now.

(She pushes him back in the chair and straddles him.)

Happy Anniversary, Senator.

(They kiss. It is good. Until **TOM***'s cell phone rings. The phone is closer to* **LISA***)*

TOM. Ignore it.

LISA. Absolutely.

TOM. Unless it's Craig.

LISA. *(glancing at the ringing phone)* It's Craig.

(She hands him the ringing phone.)

TOM. *(to* **LISA***)* One minute, I promise.

(on the phone)

Craig. I'm sitting here with my beautiful wife. Craig says Happy Anniversary. Craig, she's giving you the evil eye.

LISA. No.

TOM. She's giving me the evil eye.

LISA. Right.

TOM. So let's make this quick – what'cha got? Tell them I'm very sympathetic, but I think we should approach it through the corporate sector and I've got some ideas on how best to accomplish that. Find me ten minutes with him on Monday, I'll do the rest.

(to **LISA***)* That's why they call me Mr. Fixit. *(on the phone* Is that it? Thanks, let's talk in the morning.

(He hangs up.)

LISA. The morning, you mean, Monday? Because we have church in the morning.

TOM. Church in the morning?

LISA. Tom. You promised to go to church with me tomorrow.

TOM. Is it Easter?

LISA. You know it's not.

TOM. I'm particularly fond of Easter.

LISA. Don't tell me you forgot. Tom!

TOM. I have a conference call – it's been set up for 10:30 tomorrow.

LISA. Reschedule it, Mr. Fixit.

TOM. I can't, there are too many people involved.

LISA. Then we'll go to the eight o'clock service.

TOM. And I'm going to have to prepare for the call.

LISA. But we discussed this, I was counting on your company. I asked you especially for this weekend, for our anniversary weekend – I confirmed it with you three days ago.

TOM. I'm sorry.

LISA. Was it really that much to ask, on this weekend of all weekends?

(*TOM's phone pings. A text.*)

TOM. I'll make it up to you.

(*TOM's phone pings twice more in quick succession. **LISA** grabs the phone and starts across the room.*)

What are you doing with my phone?

LISA. Yes, what to do with your damn phone?! What would be the most satisfying demise of the wretched phone? Trash? Toilet? Garbage disposal?

(*TOM's phone rings while it is still in her hands. She answers.*)

(*into the phone*) Craig – you're new – and my husband clearly forgot to tell you the rule.

TOM. I did, I forgot.

LISA. We don't work on our anniversary. Unless it's an emergency, is it an emergency? Good. *(to* **TOM***)* The Union is safe. *(on the phone)* Can I relay a message to the Senator for you? Uh-huh. Oh, really. *(to* **TOM***)* He says Governor Jenkins is making an ass of himself on CNN.

TOM. What?

(She hands him the phone.)

(on the phone) Let's not refer to the nominee as an 'ass.' *(looking at* **LISA***)* Ah.

LISA. I might have paraphrased.

TOM. *(on the phone)* So, what's he saying? That's not good. Yeah, send me the link, I'll watch it later.

(He hangs up.)

Craig doesn't know your sense of humor. He doesn't know that when you say 'ass' you really mean –

LISA. Jack-ass?

TOM. Let's just say, Jenkins misspoke.

LISA. Again.

TOM. Again.

LISA. As my Nana used to say, the man doesn't have the sense God gave a box of hair.

TOM. Lisa, like it or not, he's our party's nominee.

LISA. Yes, and you know what that means? It means for the second time in my life I'm voting for the Democrat.

TOM. You're going to take that back.

LISA. No.

(He grabs her.)

And that's not all – stop it, Tommy – I'm going to vote all Democrat all down the – stop now, Tommy, stop, I take it back – I take it back!

(She is now in his lap.)

TOM. I'm sorry about church tomorrow.

LISA. —

TOM. I really am.

LISA. I don't think you forgot.

TOM. …You can't force it, Lisa.

LISA. I'm sorry, that was not my intent.

TOM. Wasn't it?

LISA. I've never tried to force you.

TOM. Lately, it feels like you have.

LISA. Lately I've been lonely, Tommy!

(She extracts herself and goes to the door.)

TOM. Hey…

LISA. I'm going to go for a run before it gets too hot.

TOM. Don't leave now.

LISA. I'll make the cake when I get back and then we can call Maddie.

TOM. Lisa.

LISA. *(The words tumble out.)* As for this evening, why don't you start the grill around 6:30, then we'll watch the game and have cake – I thought I'd do coconut for the cake, I've always wanted to try coconut and this year there's no reason not to, so…

(He goes to her and takes her in his arms. She holds on tight. After a beat:)

TOM. Close your eyes.

(He gets a wrapped gift out of his desk drawer. She opens it to find a framed photo.)

LISA. Oh…

TOM. Do you remember when that was taken?

LISA. Of course. Look how young. And handsome.

TOM. Why, thank you.

LISA. Not you. The waiter.

TOM. Of course.

LISA. …I love it, thank you.

TOM. You're the best part of my life. You and Maddie.

LISA. Me too.

TOM. What do you say we renew our vows this year? When Maddie gets back from camp.

LISA. —

TOM. Will you marry me again, Lisa Christine Trevor?

LISA. …Yes. Always.

(He kisses her.)

(Lights shift. Several hours later. **TOM** *is handing* **MATT** *a beer.)*

TOM. Your candidate has to stop making all these unforced errors.

MATT. My candidate? Jenkins is your candidate, too.

TOM. But I don't work for him. Look, he's smart, his budget plan is just shy of brilliant –

MATT. It is brilliant.

TOM. But who's advising him on trade? Because he doesn't seem to understand the distinction between supporting the kinds of technology initiatives that – sorry, you just got here –

(passing a dish)

Nice to see you, have a peanut!

MATT. The trade gaffe was unfortunate / and –

TOM. It's not a gaffe if he keeps doing it.

MATT. He doesn't keep doing it. The media keeps replaying it.

TOM. I get you, but Jenkins still needs to articulate a coherent trade and energy policy. I would be willing to sit down with him – in fact I would like to sit down with him – I'm assuming this is what you came to talk to me about.

MATT. That's part of it, yes.

TOM. Good, because I think I can help him and he needs it.

LISA. *(offstage)* Tom?

TOM. *(calling)* In here! *(to* **MATT***)* I should probably warn you.

MATT. Warn me about what?

TOM. Lisa's not going to be happy you're here.

MATT. What?

TOM. She may be a little prickly.

MATT. Prickly?

TOM. Okay more like angry.

MATT. Angry?

TOM. Just at first.

MATT. But –

TOM. I'm sure she'll melt the very second she sees you.

LISA. *(offstage)* No one had powdered sugar!

 (entering)

 I had to go to three different… *(noticing* **MATT***)* stores.

MATT. There she is!

LISA. Matt.

MATT. Lisa – I'm so glad to see you, how are you?

LISA. I'm just fine, Matthew, how are you?

MATT. *(handing* **LISA** *a gorgeous bouquet)* Happy anniversary.

TOM. How about that? He brought us flowers.

MATT. I brought *her* flowers.

TOM. He brought you flowers.

LISA. Aren't you sweet, isn't he sweet, Tom.

TOM. Yes he is.

LISA. What brings you to town?

MATT. I've always loved Virginia in the summer.

LISA. Not even Robert E. Lee loved Virginia in the summer.

MATT. And I've missed you. Both of you.

LISA. You've missed us?

MATT. Very much.

LISA. Well! Thank you for the flowers, they're exquisite.

MATT. I'm so glad you like them, as I was saying to Tom –

LISA. And lilies were Jay's favorites, so that's particularly thoughtful.

MATT. Right, yes, that's, yes!

LISA. *(to* **TOM***)* They were your brother's favorites.

TOM. Okay.

MATT. I would also say they're my favorites – they're a very popular flower – in fact, the lady at the florist –

LISA. Did you really think you could come here and we wouldn't talk about Jay?

MATT. Not at all, no, in fact –

LISA. Never mind, let's hear about your new boyfriend instead. He's such a nice, quiet little homosexual. He'll never shame you by doing anything loud or embarrassing.

MATT. Why are you so hostile?

LISA. Why are you surprised?

TOM. Lisa.

LISA. *(to* **TOM***)* I'm sorry, but – *(to* **MATT***)* I'm sorry. I am. But this anniversary is hard enough without…

MATT. Without having me here.

LISA. You chose to work for Steve Jenkins. You are one of the most talented men in Washington and you chose to work for him. And in the process you chose to break the heart of one of the sweetest men I ever knew.

MATT. That's not why Jay and I broke up. The Governor knows I'm gay. And honestly, you would like him –

(at her expression)

Yes you would, you would like him. I agree that he's coming on pretty strong right now; it's to excite the base, it/ doesn't mean –

LISA. I don't know how you can be so blasé about something so basic to your own interests.

MATT. Because there are many more important issues to me, I'm sorry, there just are! In fact, when did *you* become such an advocate for gay rights? When we were at school, I distinctly remember the look of, of disgust on your face when you found out I was gay.

LISA. How dare you?

MATT. Listen, I got over it, we were young –

LISA. There was no look of disgust –

MATT. You tried to hide it, but that made it even worse.

(**LISA** *looks at* **TOM**.)

TOM. I don't remember anything like that.

MATT. You were at Quantico by then.

LISA. Matthew, you have no idea what I was thinking twenty-five years ago, but I bet if you try really, really hard, you can guess what I'm thinking right now.

TOM. Okay, that's it, let's start over.

MATT. *(to* LISA*)* I'm sorry. You're right. What I was trying to/ say –

LISA. *(to* TOM*)* He comes here, glad-handing us as if nothing had happened!

TOM. Matt, did you want to talk to me about something?

MATT. I want to talk to both of you, actually.

TOM. Okay.

LISA. No, it's not okay –

TOM. Lisa, give us twenty minutes –

LISA. No.

TOM. Matthew is one of our oldest friends, we are going to hear him out. Matt – go.

MATT. Here's what I was trying to say, in my thoroughly clumsy way.

TOM. We're waiting.

MATT. I – as you know, I've spent the last year advising the Governor on everything from the deficit to immigration, to, to…

(*He stops himself, changing his mind about what he wants to say.*)

MATT. *(cont.)* I'm sorry to have upset you. The last thing I wanted to do was come here and upset you. Either of you. Of course I knew we'd talk about Jay, I hoped we'd talk about Jay.

LISA. He would never have had that accident if it weren't for you.

TOM. The accident wasn't Matt's fault.

LISA. He wouldn't have been depressed and alone and driving at those crazy speeds –

TOM. You're crossing a line, Lis –

LISA. I'm crossing a line? He's working for someone who thinks Jay was an abomination.

TOM. No one says that.

LISA. Yes they do – Governor Jenkins said that. You do not get to pretend that he didn't say that.

MATT. He used that word almost ten years ago –

LISA. Your boss is using the Bible to alienate people!

MATT. He doesn't/ really –

LISA. Abomination, Matt. *Abomination?*

MATT. People change.

LISA. Matthew, we live in a world full of phonies and chicken shits and God knows this kind of behavior doesn't usually surprise me –

TOM. Jesus, Lisa.

LISA. It doesn't even always bother me. I understand you have ambitions and that you have to go along to get along –

MATT. You have no idea what you're talking about.

LISA. Really. Then I'm sure you'll be very happy to excuse me.

(**LISA** *exits.*)

MATT. Jesus *God.*

TOM. I'm sorry.

MATT. I had no idea she felt that way.

TOM. I'm not sure she really does.

MATT. I'm walking around trying to muddle through my life, and I had no idea that all this hatred was radiating at me from Central Virginia.

TOM. She doesn't hate you.

MATT. I like to think I'm good at what I do –

TOM. One of the best.

MATT. So what is it about Lisa that can just – she's so self-righteous! And I mean that in the good way.

TOM. I understand.

MATT. I seem to have fucked this whole thing up.

TOM. What thing?

MATT. *(beat)* Jenkins is going to announce his VP choice this week.

TOM. It's about time – who's it going to be? Please don't say Hollins.

MATT. He's hoping it's going to be you.

TOM. Me?

MATT. I came here to ask if you'd be willing to be vetted.

(**TOM** *laughs, then maybe* **MATT** *laughs. Maybe a lot.*)

You think I came here just for some foreign policy advice? Tom, are you really going to tell me that you didn't see this coming when I walked in the room?

TOM. With the differences in our positions? We're like Nixon and Goldwater, he and I. No, Nixon and Wallace. No, Nixon and…

MATT. Why do you always have to torture me with Nixon? Why?

TOM. I'm just saying that we have some very different outlooks.

MATT. Not that different.

TOM. Nation building? The climate?

MATT. These are differences that make you interesting. You're the guy.

TOM. He barely knows me.

MATT. He knows a lot about you, and he's impressed. Very impressed. With both you and Lisa, actually.

TOM. Lisa?

MATT. He's heard what she has done with the shelter and he wants to support it.

TOM. Support it how?

MATT. Give it a higher profile.

TOM. You're kidding, those women mean the world to Lisa.

MATT. Steve's very interested in helping out on that. And with your successes in the House and now the Senate – well, obviously that's made a lot of people sit up and take notice.

TOM. You're serious.

MATT. Think about it. It's surprising, yes – but it's smart. It's smart for us, it's smart for you – and it's smart for the party. We need you, Tom. Jenkins has allowed himself to be…distracted by some of the anti-intellectual and yes, anti-gay wing of the party – but that's not who he is.

TOM. I think we need to have this conversation when Lisa's in the room.

MATT. I agree. That was my original plan.

TOM. You really screwed that up.

MATT. I really did. *(beat)* I don't know if you knew, but, Jay and I were in touch a little, before the accident. Maybe I should mention that to Lisa.

TOM. Don't use my brother.

MATT. I'm wasn't, I was just going to –

TOM. It sounded for a moment there, that you were going to use Jay to get to Lisa. Don't.

MATT. But that's the other thing – he's your brother. I would think if anyone had the right –

TOM. Don't do that. Don't try to parse out who should feel what. He was her best friend for almost thirty years.

MATT. I know, sorry. I was just – never mind. Sorry.

TOM. It's all right.

MATT. Any advice on how I can fix it with her?

TOM. Are you the one that told Jenkins about her work at the shelter?

MATT. I may have mentioned it. Repeatedly.

(**TOM** *makes a 'you've got your answer' gesture.*)

MATT. Right. Okay.

TOM. Can I be honest with you for a second?

MATT. I should hope so.

TOM. Not politico to politico. Friend to friend.

MATT. *(uh-oh)* What is it?

TOM. Old friend to old friend.

MATT. Yes?

TOM. Debate partner to debate partner. Fraternity brother to fraternity brother, drinking buddy to drinking –

MATT. Come on!

TOM. My heart is beating a mile a minute right now.

(*They look at each other. Isn't life strange.*)

MATT. Remember when Lisa, Jay and I roadtripped to your commissioning ceremony?

TOM. Of course.

MATT. Jay said you'd be president some day.

TOM. I think he was impressed by the uniform. It made me look more consequential.

MATT. It wasn't the uniform. It was you.

TOM. Yeah, well, Jay…

MATT. He was also talking about it the last time I saw him. I got the impression it was something you had discussed.

TOM. *(beat)* Some of the Governor's positions concern me.

MATT. I understand.

TOM. Some of mine must concern him.

MATT. They *interest* him.

(**LISA** *enters and retrieves the flowers.*)

LISA. Excuse me.

MATT. Lisa, I'm glad you're back, come and sit down with us and let me explain what I came here to…

(**LISA** *exits with the flowers.*)

TOM. She's softening.

MATT. How can you tell?

TOM. I can tell.

MATT. I didn't break up with Jay because of my work for the campaign, you know that, right?

TOM. It was a big opportunity for you.

MATT. It was a game changing opportunity for me, but that's not why we broke up. It's important to me that you understand that.

TOM. I understand.

MATT. Good. Obviously, there's a lot to discuss. We'll want to talk to Lisa – if she'll let us – and if both of you are on board then you'll want to talk to your team, as well as to Maddie.

TOM. I told you, Maddie is at arts camp.

MATT. Where, the Khyber Pass?

TOM. Michigan.

MATT. I hear they have phones in Michigan.

TOM. How soon does Jenkins expect an answer?

MATT. I told him today was your anniversary, and that your anniversary is sacred. That Lisa confiscates all your devices and forwards your home phone calls to undisclosed locations.

Steve loved all that by the way, family is fundamental to him and he feels it's really important / to honor the marriage // by taking the time to nurture the bond///between –

TOM. Matt. Matt. *Matt.*

MATT. Yeah?

TOM. This isn't a press conference. It's just me you're talking to.

MATT. He can give you the weekend.

TOM. Who else is he vetting?

MATT. Just you.

TOM. C'mon.

MATT. Hollins has already been vetted; he's ready to go, he wants to serve, he's a good, solid choice.

TOM. He's a weenie.

MATT. He's a good solid choice. But Steve wants you. So, if it's a go, we'd like to set up a meeting for Monday night. Concurrently, we'll be gathering all the paperwork; I'm not anticipating any real problems, in fact there's only one issue that I can see as potentially a, a, a complication, but I certainly don't think it needs to be.

TOM. A complication?

MATT. I don't think it needs to be.

TOM. What issue is that?

MATT. I thought you wanted to wait for Lisa.

TOM. I do, but now you're suggesting there's an issue and I'm curious – what issue is that?

MATT. It's not an issue, I don't see it rising to the level of issue.

TOM. Understood, just tell me –

MATT. And I really don't see it being a problem at all in the long run.

TOM. What is it, Matt?

MATT. You need to sound more Christian.

TOM. —

MATT. In your speeches and your public statements, you need to – don't shake your head.

TOM. That's private.

MATT. Tom, if we go forward with this, there are going to be a lot of things that were once private, that aren't going to be private anymore.

TOM. I understand that, but –

MATT. I'm not sure if you do. No one does. You can say you understand, but you can't understand; not until you're in it.

TOM. They're worried about my, Christianity?

MATT. They're not worried, they'd just like to hear a little more about it from you.

TOM. Matt –

MATT. You never talk about God.

TOM. Because it's private.

MATT. You never even say, 'God bless America.'

TOM. Sure I do.

MATT. Not enough. People have noticed.

TOM. What people?

MATT. One or two of the other advisors. Bob Chase.

TOM. I have a sixty-eight percent approval rating, I assume *people* noticed that.

MATT. No need to be patronizing. So it wasn't an issue when you ran for the Senate.

TOM. No. Virginians appreciated my results in the House and my war record –

MATT. Some would say heroism.

TOM. Whatever you call it, we didn't have to get God mixed up in an election.

MATT. That's what I said, that you're just quiet about it.

TOM. If by quiet about it, you mean I'm not interested in meeting some kind of faith based litmus test, then yes, you can say I'm quiet about it.

MATT. Tom –

TOM. I would have thought that Jenkins is a vocal enough Christian to have everyone else's ass covered.

MATT. Ouch.

TOM. I am assuming the campaign is reaching out to me because as a Mid-western Governor, Jenkins would appreciate a Southern partner.

MATT. Of course.

TOM. And because I am considered a centrist, and you
need that balance too.

MATT. Yes, but c'mon, you can give them a bone! Go to
church with your wife a little more often –

TOM. I do go to church.

MATT. Christmas and Easter?

TOM. Yes, and I'm very fond of Easter. Tell them that.

MATT. Tell them you're 'fond of' Easter?

TOM. Yes.

MATT. I'm not telling them you're fond of Easter.

TOM. Listen, nothing would make Lisa happier than if I
started going to church with her on a regular basis.

MATT. So then, do it, that's all. Make Lisa happy! And while
you're at it, sprinkle around a few "I love Jesus-es" here
and there.

TOM. Matt, I don't speak that way, it doesn't – has never
come naturally to me and I...don't speak that way. If I
were to start littering my statements with God this, and
Jesus that, it would sound phony and I don't think me
sounding phony would be to anyone's benefit.

MATT. But what's wrong with referencing foundational –

TOM. If the bargain is, you need me to start talking about
God – maybe you're looking in the wrong place.

MATT. I was afraid this would sound more consequential
than it is. I shouldn't have brought it up yet. There is a
right time to do these things.

TOM. "To everything there is a season". *(beat)* As the Good
Book says.

MATT. See?! What's so hard about that? A nice psalm here,
a little Ecclesiastes there.

TOM. —

MATT. You just need to signal that you're a believer. That's
all. Quotes are good.

TOM. I don't know that I am.

MATT. What.

TOM. A believer.

MATT. You don't have to be born again, no one is saying that. Just indicate how your belief in Jesus – how your faith has been a – a foundation for the way you…

(Looking at **TOM** *more carefully. Beat.)*

Uh-oh.

TOM. I admire Jesus.

MATT. You admire Jesus?

TOM. Yes, he was a good man, wasn't he? A very good man. A great man.

MATT. You don't believe in the divinity of Christ?

TOM. Not really, no.

MATT. …Okay, please don't say that to anyone else.

TOM. I would prefer not to.

MATT. Right. So, let's just, uh…let's go back to God for a minute. You obviously believe there's a God, right, so how about if we…

(looking at **TOM** *more carefully again)*

You're kidding.

TOM. I'm not kidding, I'm an agnostic. *(helpfully)* I don't know.

MATT. I know what agnostic means!

TOM. If I'm going to be honest, I don't know about a God. In fact, I'm more inclined to think there isn't a God. But, as I say, I don't know.

MATT. But doesn't Lisa – this isn't a problem for the two of you?

TOM. We navigate it fine.

MATT. You navigate it fine?

TOM. Yes.

MATT. But how does she –

TOM. *(cutting him off)* Matt. We navigate it fine.

MATT. How the holy fuck is this news to me?!

TOM. Look, I'm not saying that faith in God is a bad thing – in fact, I think it can often be a good thing. Maddie and Lisa believe that they will see Jay again. I wish I believed that.

(a deep breath)

But I don't. And more to our point here, if my daughter didn't have a faith, or the wrong faith, or questions about faith, I don't think she should be discriminated against.

MATT. Neither do I.

TOM. Even if she wanted to, say, run for President. I think that should be separate. I think our Founders insisted on it. I mean, they couldn't all agree on something as obvious as slavery – but you know what? They did agree on this. And I'm here to tell ya, on this one I gotta go with the Founders.

MATT. Yeah Tom, that's a very pretty speech, but it's not going to fly.

TOM. It's not going to fly in the Heartland?

MATT. It's not even going to fly on the coasts!

TOM. "Question with boldness even the existence of a God."

MATT. Who said that?

TOM. That's Thomas Jefferson, baby.

MATT. Sometimes I really hate that guy.

*(staring at **TOM**, weighing his options)*

Half of my very soul is screaming for me to walk out that door, right now.

TOM. Because I doubt the existence of God? Matt.

MATT. All things being equal – I would love to have a spirited debate with you about that. Even better, I would love to have another beer and watch the game and argue over whether Barry Bonds should be in the Hall of Fame.

TOM. He should.

MATT. He should *not*, but I don't have that kind of time right now. The convention is looming –

TOM. You said only half of you wanted to walk out that door.

MATT. Between you and me, I'm not sure the Governor can win with Hollins.

TOM. I'm not sure either.

MATT. But with you on the ticket… Tom, I think this is one of those cases where it could make the difference. As long as –

TOM. As long as I sprinkle a little God stuff here and there.

MATT. (**MATT** *takes out his buzzing cell and glances at it.*) Sorry – I need to take care of this one. It shouldn't take long.

TOM. I'll give you some privacy. I have to take care of a few things myself.

MATT. *(into the phone)* Yeah, hold on a sec. *(covering the phone)* I think you want this, Tom. So let's figure out how to make it work.

(**TOM** *exits without answering.*)

(into phone) What's going on? We've just started, but it looks good! What do ya got for me? I don't want Steve on *Meet The Press* next week, it's not the best arena for him right now, put them off, tell them after the convention he'd love to do it – what else? Eric can handle that – what else? Okay, yeah, I'll send them an email, what else? You're kidding me, please tell me you are kidding me. Tell them the Governor loves eggs, he just doesn't like them scrambled. I don't know, he likes egg salad and, and quiche, he likes quiche – no don't say quiche. Look, we're not apologizing – no, tell the United Egg Producers they can go fuck themselves! But not in those words. Thanks.

(**MATT** *turns to see that* **LISA** *has entered. She has the flowers arranged beautifully in a vase)*

Apparently Steve has offended the egg lobby.

LISA. *(an overture)* He'll never win without the egg lobby.

> *(Beat. It's awkward.* LISA *puts the flowers on a side table.)*

> It's always so dark in this corner of the room, isn't it, I mean, it's not even five o'clock but you can barely –

> *(She attempts to turn on a lamp but when she pulls the lamp chain, it comes off in her hands.)*

> *(under her breath)* Damn-it!

> *(glancing at* **MATT***)*

> I hate this hideous lamp. But it was Jay's, so, you know, I kind of love it too.

> *(They consider each other. It's still awkward. Then –)*

MATT. I'm sorry about before, it was rude of me to just – what?

LISA. *(overlapping)* Can you please tell me how I have the nerve to ever – what?

MATT. You first.

LISA. I just, I'm wondering how I have the nerve to – ever – question why the Israelis and the Palestinians can't 'get along.' When here I am, in my own home, making a colossal mess of things. With people I love.

MATT. Did you say, people you love?

LISA. Yes. Of course yes.

MATT. I love you too.

LISA. Then why have you been such a stranger?

MATT. I haven't; I tried to get in touch, I sent you some emails.

LISA. Two.

MATT. Yes two. That you never answered.

LISA. Two emails.

MATT. That you never answered.

LISA. It's been over a year since you broke up with Jay. Two emails?

MATT. To be fair, they were more letter than email –

LISA. You break up with Jay, you take up with that other boy –

MATT. Michael.

LISA. Jay has the accident, we barely see you at the funeral and with all these monumental events, two emails? Two emails?

MATT. That you never answered!

LISA. Oh my God, Matt!

MATT. But why is it only my responsibility – !!

LISA. Because you broke up with us!! So you have to work harder to get us back!! *(beat)* That sounded kind of dumb.

MATT. No, it sounded kind of right. Breaking up with Jay was like breaking up with all of you.

LISA. I don't believe the accident was your fault. That was a horrible thing to say. The look on your face, when I said that. I'm so sorry.

MATT. Thank you.

LISA. Jay was driving too fast because he loved driving fast. That's all. It was just, it was senseless. You know? Completely and stupidly, senseless. Matt, I'm so glad you're here. I've missed you so much. Can I tell you something? We've been struggling.

MATT. What do you mean, struggling?

LISA. You know that I pray, all the time. It's second nature for me, to be in constant conversation with God. But after the accident…it wasn't that I hated God – I just wondered if He was even *there.* And if He wasn't there…then what? My pastor said, when you're having that kind of trouble, 'Look for the helpers. God is in the helpers.' So I thought about the stranger who wouldn't leave Jay's side in the ambulance. And the policeman who called us, who had just the right voice, somehow, to tell us that news. And little by little God's stubborn grace kept finding me again. But not Tom.

Tom won't even talk about it. The last four months he's... Tom needs a friend, a real friend. There aren't enough people he can trust in this business. He needs you.

MATT. He's got me.

LISA. I need you too.

MATT. Of course – always.

LISA. Really?

MATT. Do you even need to ask?

LISA. Because you said earlier, that I looked at you with disgust.

MATT. No, I – no, it was twenty-five years ago, I'm sure I got it/ wrong –

LISA. I don't think it was disgust, exactly, but it was something.

MATT. You had a crush on me.

LISA. Oh, get over yourself!

MATT. It's true.

LISA. Everyone had a crush on you, you...dope.

MATT. Including you.

LISA. Yes, including me, big secret revealed! But no, when you told me, it was...maybe it was a kind of... I was shocked, I was. I was shocked and I was uncomfortable and that's just the truth. I think it was different with Jay because, I guess because he was always so up front about it. There was no disconnect. But Matt – you worked so hard to hide it.

MATT. I didn't work 'so hard' –

LISA. You dated more beautiful women than any other guy on that campus! And then it turned out it was all for show. You didn't have to work that hard. You still don't have to work that hard.

MATT. Believe me, I work hard at many, many things. But not that.

LISA. Does Jenkins ask you about your boyfriend, show interest in your life with Michael?

MATT. No.

LISA. See, I don't like that. He should ask.

MATT. He doesn't ask because we broke up.

> *(at her expression)*

> No, not because of Jenkins. Because I have no time and Michael wanted more of a partner. This is who I am, Lisa. I don't have a personal life.

LISA. And yet you've taken this whole day to come to Richmond and visit with Tom and me. That means so much to us, thank you, thank you, Matt. A whole day during the campaign? How did you even get Jenkins to spare you? With only, what, two weeks before the *(a realization)* convention…

MATT. Right.

LISA. Oh no. *(incredulous)* Does Jenkins want Tom to be his running mate?

MATT. There's obviously a lot to talk about.

LISA. Jenkins?

MATT. Including some things that I think you'll find particularly exciting.

LISA. *Jenkins?*

MATT. I'm telling you, you have the wrong idea about him.

LISA. What did Tom say?

MATT. We wanted to wait for you.

LISA. What did he say, Matt?

MATT. He brought up Nixon.

LISA. Of course he did.

MATT. I was really hoping he would have grown out of that –

LISA. No, it's gotten worse.

MATT. It's like he has Tourettes, Nixonian Tourettes. It's like he has some rare mental disorder known as, what, known as…

LISA. Acute Intermittent Nixonmania.

MATT. Yes! You are a genius, a beautiful genius. And for the record? I had a crush on you too.

LISA. —

MATT. So. I guess we should go find Tom, and, figure this out?

(**MATT** *goes to the door.* **LISA** *has not moved.*)

MATT. Are you coming?

LISA. All joking aside.

MATT. What is it?

LISA. Tom is a good man.

MATT. That's why the Nixon love is so mystifying to me.

LISA. No, Matt. Listen to me. Tom is a good man.

MATT. Yes he is. And?

LISA. And he's navigating the Senate pretty well, as far as that goes.

MATT. I know there's a point here, but I'm not sure what it is.

LISA. Then I'm just going to say it.

MATT. Great!

LISA. The arena you're playing in – at this presidential level – when you take good people and put them in that, snake pit –

MATT. Jesus, Lisa, could you at least try to be a little less insulting? We need good people. We are desperate for good people. And they are out there, and Tom is one of them.

LISA. Yes, and I want him to stay one of them.

MATT. Tom is not going to change in any kind of fundamental way.

LISA. How do you know?

MATT. How do I know? What are you getting at?

LISA. Nothing.

MATT. I know because Tom is one of the most straight up guys on the planet.

LISA. —

MATT. Isn't he?

LISA. Yes.

MATT. Is he?!

LISA. Yes! Of course, yes. But there are –

MATT. I already know about the God problem.

LISA. The God problem. See, already you make it sound so crass.

MATT. I'm just saying it doesn't have to be a deal breaker.

LISA. Maybe not in *Russia*.

MATT. Was it an issue in the Senate race?

LISA. No, it wasn't; Tom is a star. Besides, I think people assume certain things, Virginians know me and what I do, and they assume certain things. But I'm betting a presidential race is going to be different.

MATT. You've thought about this.

LISA. You bet your ass I have.

MATT. Good, that's good. But for now –

LISA. Where is he right now?

MATT. I don't know, I had a call and he left the room, why?

LISA. Because he's probably already putting things in motion, calling his team – he's ambitious, Matt.

MATT. Of course he is, and he should be.

LISA. Tom can't be in a national campaign. Not with his "God problem."

MATT. Let's just take one step at a time. Can we do that?

LISA. Tom can't be in a national campaign.

MATT. Lisa. Please?

(**LISA** *walks to the window and looks out at the backyard.*)

LISA. …Jay started going to church before he died. I didn't know if he'd told you.

MATT. No.

LISA. He wanted to know God, Matt. He found this church he liked and he asked me to go with him, so I switched. To St. Mark's Episcopal. They're more formal than I'm used to but, Jay was really taken with them there so…

MATT. I know how much that means to you.

LISA. We planted that tree for him.

MATT. What tree?

LISA. The dogwood. By the wall.

MATT. You mean that stick?

LISA. It's a sapling.

MATT. What happened to the leaves?

LISA. They got stressed. But they're growing back. They are. Don't laugh.

MATT. You say everyone was in love with me in college, but in the real world it was Jay who had to beat the guys off with a stick.

LISA. But he loved you.

(beat)

Matt? What is it?

MATT. Sometimes I wonder if anyone will ever –

LISA. They will.

MATT. I don't know. I think Jay was it. I miss him, Lisa. And you and Tom – you're my family. You're the only family that ever mattered to me.

LISA. We're still here.

(TOM enters.)

TOM. You're probably wondering where/ I've…

MATT. (holding up his cell) Excuse me, I have to return some calls.

(MATT leaves abruptly.)

TOM. Is Matt all right?

LISA. He misses Jay.

TOM. Do you think I should… (motions as if to follow MATT.)

LISA. I think you should give him a minute.

(**TOM** *nods.*)

LISA. I don't want to do it, Tom.

TOM. He told you about Jenkins?

LISA. I don't want to do it.

TOM. Let's just hear what he has to say –

LISA. No. Let's not. Let's be grateful to have Matt back in our lives. Let's just have dinner together and, and pretend we're twenty-one again.

TOM. Lisa, I have just been asked to run for the vice presidency of the United States of America – the most powerful country on the planet. Not for nothin', Honey, but don't you want to, I don't know, admire me for a moment?

LISA. I do, I do admire you.

TOM. Then don't you think it's possible/ that –

LISA. You can't run for that office, Tom. I can see you want to, but you can't. You can't run for vice president and not believe in God. They won't let you. They will tear you apart.

TOM. No one's going to tear me apart.

LISA. Better you had been a former drug addict than not believe in God. Better you had had multiple affairs, exaggerated your military service, kicked small dogs, sent pictures of your penis across Twitter.

(*She has noticed* **TOM** *tapping his watch urgently.*)

What? Oh – what time is it, what time is it?

TOM. It's almost five.

LISA. What time is it exactly?

TOM. It's 4:59 and…exactly fifty-four seconds. fifty-five, fifty-six –

LISA & TOM. Fifty-seven, fifty-eight, fifty-nine…

LISA. Twenty years ago, Tommy.

TOM. Twenty years ago *exactly.*

(*He kisses her, then –*)

I'd better go check on Jay *(correcting himself)* – Matt.

*(***TOM*** *goes to the door.)*

LISA. I'm scared, Tommy.

TOM. *(stopped in his tracks)* Scared?

LISA. This thing…it feels like a bad idea for us. Please don't do this. Please.

TOM. All we're doing is hearing him out. There's no harm in that, right?

LISA. —

TOM. *(definitive)* There's no harm in it.

(as he is exiting)

LISA. Tom, wait.

TOM. Nothing is going to happen that we both don't agree on.

LISA. —

TOM. Hey. Hey pretty girl. We're in this together. I promise.

LISA. Are we?

TOM. *(trying – but not quite succeeding – to hide his impatience)* I promise.

*(***TOM*** *exits.* ***LISA*** *looks out into the yard a moment, then holds up her hands – palms out – in prayer.)*

(Lights shift.)

End of Act One

ACT TWO

(Later. **TOM** *and* **MATT**. *There is an empty container of peanuts.)*

MATT. Have you ever paid for sex?

Do you watch internet porn?

Could there be a sex-tape out there – even if it's with your wife?

TOM. These are probing questions, Matt.

MATT. Is there anything in your past that might make you vulnerable to blackmail or coercion? Have you ever sent an electronic communication, including but not limited to email, text, Instagram, or Twitter that could suggest a conflict of interest or be a possible source of embarrassment to you?

TOM. Okay, so/ if I –

MATT. What will your high school algebra teacher say about you? Have you ever had a DUI? Or electroshock therapy? Oh, and you do know there's two Koreas, don't you?

TOM. I've heard that in these situations you feel compelled to confess things. Every "B-" in Organic Chemistry, every unkind word.

MATT. What do you feel compelled to confess?

TOM. That "B-" in Organic Chemistry.

MATT. We already know about that.

(at **TOM***'s expression)*

I'm not joking.

TOM. You know who should have vetted his VP a little more carefully?

MATT. Please don't go there. Again.

TOM. All we seem to remember are the mistakes – I'd like to celebrate the successes! He established the Environmental Protection Agency, OSHA, the Consumer Product Safety Commission –

(**LISA** *enters.*)

He eradicated the gold standard – Hi Hon.

LISA. *(to* **MATT***)* Nixon?

MATT. Nixon.

TOM. And I haven't even mentioned China, yet. Or Détente!

LISA. *(to* **MATT***)* What happened here? I leave you alone with him for half an hour.

MATT. I lost focus for a second and he pounced.

TOM. During his presidency we walked on the moon. He placed a phone call to Neil Armstrong. On the moon.

LISA. *(to* **MATT***)* He's just trying to annoy us.

TOM. I don't understand how people can be so blasé about the moon.

MATT. *(to* **LISA***)* Don't let him know it's working.

TOM. The two of you are, yes, you're very amusing, but you cannot deny that if it wasn't for Watergate, Nixon would be considered one of the most/ effective –

MATT. If it wasn't for that, Mrs. Lincoln, how did you like the play?

TOM. I agree, Watergate was bad.

MATT. Way to go out on a limb there, Tommy.

TOM. And yes, it keeps him out of the Hall of Fame and yes, that is appropriate.

MATT. I guess you could say he's the Barry Bonds of presidents.

TOM. Thank you, that's it! He had a great Presidency, except for –

MATT. Except for that one thing.

TOM. And Barry Bonds was one of the greatest hitters of all time, and since he wasn't actually convicted of the drugs –

MATT. Just the lying about it.

TOM. True, but if you stopped Bonds' career before all that he is still a hall of fame/ hitter.

MATT. Before 'all that'? You can't just pick and choose/ whatever you –

LISA. *Gentlemen!* It is my twentieth wedding anniversary and no one has offered me a drink.

TOM. Honey, I'm sorry. Can I get you some wine? I opened the Montrachet.

LISA. Yes, please.

TOM. Matt?

MATT. I've still got my beer.

(*As* **TOM** *pours* **LISA** *her wine, she notices the lamp.*)

LISA. Oh, Tommy! You fixed the lamp.

TOM. Like I keep saying – that's why they call me –

LISA. Mr. Fixit, I know.

(**TOM** *hands* **LISA** *her wine.*)

So before we get into all this, stuff – you fellas are probably hungry – Tom, should we start the grill?

TOM. Not hungry.

LISA. Not hungry?

MATT. We ate the peanuts.

LISA. All the peanuts?

TOM. We're sorry.

LISA. But there was a *pound.*

MATT. We're very sorry.

LISA. Over a pound of peanuts!

MATT. The best thing about Virginia is those Virginia peanuts.

LISA. I beg your pardon?

MATT. No, you're right. The best thing about Virginia is you. *(to* **TOM***)* And even you. So I'd like to make a toast. To Tom and Lisa, still the truest people I know. I have always been my best self with you, thank you for that. And thank you for the inspiration of your incredible, beautiful partnership. I wish…it feels like home being here with you again. Happy Anniversary.

LISA. Thank you, Matthew.

TOM. Yes, congratulations, you've succeeded in embarrassing me to such a degree that I feel the need to remind you that even Richard Nixon – as a young lad on his father's lemon farm in Yorba Linda, California –

(Pleased with their reaction, **TOM** *raises his glass.)*

To family.

LISA & MATT. To family.

MATT. Remember that first time Jay brought me to meet your parents? How nervous I was? I hadn't come out to my own family, yet here I was spending Thanksgiving in the Deep South.

TOM. *(an old argument)* Richmond is not the Deep South.

MATT. I even boned up on my military history just to distract your Dad.

TOM. Thanks to you, I still know more than I ever care to about naval artillery in the Golden Age of Sail. Dad was pleased though.

MATT. He knew all about it already.

TOM. Yeah, well, you were never going to 'out artillery' Dad.

MATT. No, I wasn't. Good guy.

LISA. Yes he was.

TOM. Dad always used to say that it was obvious from the beginning, from when Jay first started grade school, that he was different. You know this, right?

MATT. I do.

TOM. Jay would walk into a room and everyone would know immediately – *immediately* – that he was…a Democrat.

LISA. He could never hide it.

MATT. No, he couldn't.

(*The doorbell rings.*)

Are you expecting anyone?

TOM. No. (*to* **LISA**) I'll get it.

MATT. Tom – if it's the press…

LISA. The press?

MATT. Doubtful, but you never know. Tom?

TOM. Got it.

(**TOM** *exits.*)

LISA. The press?

MATT. I sincerely doubt it.

LISA. Oh my God…

MATT. Obviously if we do this, the Governor would like to roll it out in his own way, and not get pre-empted by some eager-beaver journalist.

LISA. And if we don't do this?

MATT. Then we don't want a story.

(**TOM** *enters and hands* **LISA** *a small plastic baggie and a note.*)

LISA. What's that?

TOM. It was left on the stoop, looks like a bracelet. It's from Tanya.

LISA. Tanya?!

(**LISA** *runs out the door.*)

TOM. (*calling out after her*) She's not there!

MATT. Tanya?

TOM. One of the girls from the shelter. Lisa found her in Monroe Park, the Mom had kicked her out, it was March and apparently she just wanted to die. And she might have, a couple people died that night in the parks. She's given Lisa nothing but grief, I have to say.

(**LISA** *enters.*)

LISA. Did you see her?

TOM. No, there was no one there.

(**LISA** *holds out the note.*)

LISA. "Happy anniversary, Mrs. T."

TOM. Nice.

LISA. Just when you think that you couldn't be a bigger failure – sometimes that's exactly when the Lord shines a light…(*fingering the bracelet*).

MATT. This reminds me, Lisa, I was talking to Steve about what you've/ been able to –

LISA. (*suddenly*) I didn't vote for him in the primary.

MATT. I understand.

LISA. And if anyone asks me, I'm not going to lie.

MATT. Nobody wants you to.

LISA. (*triumphant*) Tom didn't vote for him either.

TOM. True.

MATT. We all recognize that this is an odd marriage.

LISA. *Is?*

MATT. Would be. Would be an odd marriage. If it comes to pass.

LISA. Which begs the question – and Tom, forgive me Honey – but what does Tom bring to the table, in Jenkins' view?

MATT. He sees Tom as high risk, high reward.

TOM. That's how Lisa sees me too.

LISA. Very funny. (*to **MATT***) And what exactly does he want from him?

MATT. First of all, he admires that Tom is his own man. That while he's solid on the core issues, he polls well with Independents and even a good number of Democrats (*to **TOM***) He appreciates your expertise in the area of foreign policy and – well, Tom, let me ask you: If you could bring one issue to the forefront of the national conversation, what would it be?

TOM. Our energy security – because our national security is always going to be bound by our energy security – which is still too volatile. We need to continue the push toward self-sufficiency and we have to come up with an actionable plan to deal with the issue of, I hate to say it –

MATT. Climate change.

TOM. You heard my speech.

MATT. Your speech practically caused a riot at the Heritage Foundation.

TOM. Which is why it never occurred to me that Jenkins would look to me as a possible running mate. Because I haven't been shy about saying we need to get our heads out of the sand on this.

MATT. The Governor wants you to bring that into the national debate.

LISA. Really.

TOM. I thought Jenkins was kind of indifferent to the issue of climate change.

MATT. That's not true –

TOM. A lot of his supporters don't even think it's a reality.

MATT. Some of his supporters.

TOM. Or they think it's not our responsibility –

LISA. Which surprises me, because it's right there in Scripture.

TOM. Not to mention right there in Science.

MATT. Wait a second, go on, Lisa.

LISA. We are called to be the stewards of the earth. Scripture says, if I love and serve God, I have to love and serve his creation.

MATT. See! You two make a great team! And I'm thinking, if you blend the 'stewards of the earth' with the science, there's something in it for everyone.

TOM. When you say, "bring it into the national conversation," are you seriously suggesting that/ Jenkins –

MATT. Look, people may think that your opinions on climate change are a liability for us – but I have convinced Steve that we – our position is we embrace it, we don't run away from it. The Governor is not a cautious person. It doesn't mean he agrees with you by the way, but he's not afraid of the debate. And I don't think you are either, I think you want that debate.

TOM. I do. We need to frame it just right, obviously.

LISA. Wait, you're talking about this/ like it's –

MATT. I think we can pull it off.

LISA. Like it's a done deal.

TOM. Climate change is a national security issue and if that's not obvious to ninety percent of the public now, it will be soon enough.

MATT. Do you agree with that Lisa?

LISA. Yes, yes I do, but –

TOM. I've been talking to a lot of young people. The next generation knows that climate change is real and they want something done about it.

LISA. Wait – wait – wait –

TOM. The earth's temperature is changing and whether you think it's man-made or cyclical, the country that develops the most abundant sources of renewable energy will have a permanent competitive advantage. America should be that country – we *have* to be that country.

LISA. Tom, you're moving way too fast.

TOM. I'm just thinking out loud, same as I always do.

LISA. Yes, but we need to talk about the elephant in the room.

TOM. *(to* **MATT***)* This is the race to space for the foreseeable future.

MATT. Exactly, but it's how we bring in the private sector that/ will determine –

LISA. Excuse me Matt, but how would the campaign handle the faith issue?

MATT. The faith issue.

LISA. As you know, Tom is not comfortable talking about his faith –

TOM. Or lack of it.

LISA. …So how does the Governor plan to/ navigate the –

MATT. We don't need to bring him in on this yet.

LISA. But isn't he going to want to know? Isn't he going to want Tom to say certain things and –

MATT. Like I said before, one thing at a time.

LISA. But if now is not the time, when is? What are you waiting for? The interview with Hannity, when Tom is casually asked about the source of his faith and he –

TOM. *(to* **LISA***)* I would say that *you* are the source of my faith. Obviously.

LISA. Or he's invited to speak at the Southern Baptist Convention, and –

MATT. Steve will represent the campaign at the Southern Baptist Convention.

LISA. But you know what I mean, Matt! It's only a matter of time.

MATT. Tom?

LISA. Tom doesn't worry about these things. He has this belief in himself, this preternatural confidence that he can handle whatever is thrown at him – and it could get him in trouble.

MATT. I will say this, *(to* **TOM***)* and please don't fly off the handle: You can be the climate change guy, and talk about it as a Christian.

LISA. But he's not a Christian!

MATT. In Christian terms. Stewardship, God's creation –

TOM. *(to* **MATT***)* Is Jenkins honestly open to a real discussion on the climate issue?

MATT. Yes.

LISA. Wait –

TOM. A real and ongoing discussion.

MATT. *Yes.* I just happen to think we have a better chance if you talk about it like Lisa does, in the context of the Bible – in addition to the Science, of course.

LISA. Tom is not going to start quoting Scripture! He doesn't believe in it and he's not going to quote it.

MATT. *(to* **TOM***)* You can think of it like quoting any great piece of literature, like quoting Shakespeare, or Lincoln, or –

LISA. NO.

MATT. What's wrong with talking about big ideas in the context of – whether you believe in it or not, Tom – in the context of the single most important book on the planet.

LISA. Because it's not just a book! It is the Word of God and it is sacred!

MATT. I understand, but –

LISA. You don't lightly toss around His Word. And you never, never – not in this family, anyway – pull out passages to serve a political agenda. No.

TOM. But Lisa –

LISA. *(to* **MATT***)* It's not the same as quoting Shakespeare or Lincoln, or, or Thomas *Jefferson.*

MATT. I didn't mean to suggest that it's the same, I just meant, for the purposes of –

LISA. I know what you meant.

TOM. Hey, how about if I quote Jefferson quoting the Bible?

LISA. Was that supposed to be funny?

TOM. Yeah, it kind of was.

LISA. Well, it kind of was*n't.*

TOM. But it does bring up a valid point, at least to me. *(to* **MATT***)* Thomas Jefferson did not believe that Jesus was divine, either.

MATT. What are you trying to say?

TOM. Exactly that. Jefferson did not believe that Jesus Christ was the son of God. But this did not keep him from quoting Jesus. Or from quoting the Bible. Actually, here's an interesting fact – Jefferson made his own bible. He did! He literally, with a razor, cut and pasted his own bible. He left out all the miracles: no virgin birth, no resurrection: he cut out all that abracadabra and hocus-pocus –

(**LISA** *gasps.*)

His words, Lisa, his words – and he made a bible of what Jesus actually said. And this is my point: what Jesus actually said – and did – was pretty damn great.

MATT. Yeah, but the thing that worries me, Tom, is whether you can refrain from getting engaged in a debate about this. I mean, debunking one of the favorite founding fathers by saying he didn't believe that Jesus was divine –

TOM. I am not debunking Jefferson. I obviously agree with Jefferson. But give me credit for a little judgment, Matt. This is my home, and I hope that I can say what I like, in my own home.

MATT. But I worry that your delight in the 'interesting fact' –

TOM. And this is my wife, Lisa, whom I believe you know. And there is no one – no one – I respect more, but because of that, there is also no one that I can be as unfiltered with. We enjoy sparring –

(*glancing at* **LISA**, *who has retreated to a different part of the room*)

Sometimes we enjoy it more than other times – but she helps me see the world with different eyes, and I hope that I do the same for her. And because you're here, and on such an occasion, you get the benefit of things that I would not say outside of these walls. Not because I'm ashamed of them, but because they're private. It is not my neighbors' business what I believe. In fact, it was Jefferson who said it best, "It does me no injury if my neighbor says there are twenty gods – or – no god. It neither picks my pocket nor breaks my leg."

MATT. It may do you no injury, but you're not going to see that neighbor being elected vice president any time soon. However, I think we're probably giving this more weight than it deserves right now –

TOM. I agree.

LISA. Unbelievable.

TOM. Lisa –

LISA. Am I the only one who can see two steps ahead here? You guys are the politicos, not me! *(to MATT)* I can't believe that you would compromise your candidate in that way.

MATT. Lisa, I'm not going to compromise the Governor, believe me. I would never work in Washington again if I kept the kind of secret that would damage him. But I just found out about all this one hour ago, and I'm still figuring out how to handle it. And while our time is short, it's not *that* short. We have the weekend and I would prefer to –

LISA. *(stiffly formal)* Would anyone else care for some cake?

MATT. What?

LISA. I would like some cake now. Tom? Cake?

TOM. Cake?

LISA. Yes. I want cake.

TOM. We usually have it, after dinner.

LISA. I want it now.

TOM. Okay…

LISA. You saw fit to spoil your appetite with a pound of peanuts. I want cake. Cake makes me feel good. I will have cake.

(She goes to leave.)

TOM. Lisa, come back.

LISA. *(turning on him)* You called the resurrection 'hocus-pocus.'

TOM. I'm sorry, I was just using Jefferson's words.

LISA. Do you think you can just say 'nigger' or 'faggot' because someone else did?

TOM. Of course not.

LISA. Quoting someone else does not give you a free pass.

TOM. You're right.

LISA. *(upset)* Do not ever, ever refer to the Lord's resurrection as hocus-pocus.

*(There is a sudden, loud 'pop.' **LISA** cries out and instinctively moves to **TOM**. They all look to the window.)*

MATT. What the hell was that?

TOM. Might have been a bird. Flying into the window.

LISA. Oh, that scared me.

*(**TOM** goes to the window, peers at the ground.)*

TOM. I can't see anything. I'll go check.

*(First he goes to **LISA**.)*

I'm sorry. I didn't mean to hurt you.

*(**TOM** exits.)*

MATT. A bird can make that kind of noise, just hitting the window?

LISA. Yes.

MATT. But wouldn't there be a mark on the window? I don't see a mark.

LISA. Not necessarily.

MATT. And a dead bird on the ground? I don't see a bird.

LISA. Can you imagine if Tom became a lightning rod? For crazy fringe, End-of-the-Worlders? What if Tom were to be president someday? If people found out he didn't believe in God, someone would try to kill him. They would, someone would try to kill him. These situations, they bring out all the nuts, don't you think?

MATT. I think you're getting way ahead of yourself.

LISA. That's my job!

MATT. Look, I understand how overwhelming all this can be.

LISA. And what about Maddie? Maddie would have to have secret service, for how long?

MATT. Only if you win.

LISA. I've watched what campaigns do to families.

MATT. It's a challenging process.

LISA. Challenging? It's brutal! You need to give up your suit here. Tell Tom it was a bad idea, and go back to Jenkins and, and say thank you, but Tom has other priorities. Tell him we're very grateful, but –

MATT. Lisa, I'm sorry. This is something Tom has to decide.

LISA. With me!

MATT. Yes. Yes, of course with you. But you know what? I think Jay would have wanted it. Not that that's the reason to do it, but I was thinking about this, on my way down here. Jay would be thrilled, wouldn't he?

LISA. Would he?

MATT. You know he would.

LISA. Not with this candidate, I don't think so.

(**TOM** *enters, a small bird cupped gently in his hands.*)

TOM. No vandals, just a bird.

LISA. Oh, Tom…

MATT. Is it alive?

TOM. *(in wonder and fascination)* Yeah. He's still breathing. He's probably just stunned.

(**TOM** *and* **LISA** *look at the bird in* **TOM***'s hands.* **MATT** *hangs back.* **LISA** *gently strokes the bird.*)

MATT. And…what do we do now? Just, let it, wake up? Or, what?

TOM. We can't keep it inside.

LISA. We don't know how badly it's injured.

TOM. And it would hurt itself, trying to get out again.

MATT. Can't you just leave it on the ground? Outside on the ground?

TOM. Not with that serial killer running loose.

MATT. Serial killer?

LISA. Fluffy.

TOM. Fluffy lives next door.

LISA. Fluffy likes to eat birds.

TOM. Fluffy must be stopped.

> *(They all look at the bird again. Beautiful creature.)*

Maybe I should just –

TOM & LISA. Run him to the vet.

TOM. Do you mind?

LISA. Of course not.

TOM. *(to MATT)* He's just five minutes away. You want to
come?

MATT. To the vet?

TOM. We won't stay, we'll just drop him off.

MATT. In the car?

TOM. Yeah, it's just five minutes away.

MATT. But what if he wakes up? While we're still in the car?

TOM. We want him to wake up.

MATT. But what if he starts flapping around, and you know,
flaps around? When we're in the car?

TOM. You don't have to come.

MATT. No, I'll come. I just thought we should consider the
various, you know. Be prepared.

TOM. For flapping.

MATT. Yes.

LISA. I'll go find a shoe box.

MATT & TOM. Thank you.

MATT. It's just good to be prepared.

TOM. I agree.

MATT. *(trying to recover his dignity)* So, what is it? A bluebird,
right? It's so blue.

> *(**LISA** pauses at the door and watches a moment before
> leaving. This is the **TOM** she loves.)*

TOM. No, a bluebird has the vivid blue on the head and the back, while the breast is reddish-brown. This is an Indigo Bunting.

MATT. Is it rare?

TOM. No, not really. Not here, anyway. Although as the planet is warming, migratory patterns are changing; so who knows what the future will bring for these little guys…

(very moved)

Extraordinary creatures. Even the common ones, even the 'everyday' ones. Extraordinary. Hey, here's an interesting fact. Did you know that the Indigo uses the night sky as a kind of map? When the Indigo is a young bird, still in its nest, it studies the constellations, so that when it is all grown up and needs to get from say, Memphis to Belize, it can migrate at night – using what it learned as that little chick gazing up at the heavens.

MATT. That's, pretty amazing.

TOM. *(pleased)* It really is. I love birds.

MATT. I find them disturbing.

TOM. *(Maybe he laughs, and maybe he needed to.)* You're afraid of birds.

MATT. No. Okay, yes. But only when they're in an enclosed space. Outside is good. I like birds when they're outside. In trees. In the sky. I love birds in the sky.

TOM. How did I not know you were afraid of birds?

MATT. How did I not know you don't believe in God? Our friends keep things from us, it seems.

TOM. You've risked a lot for this, haven't you?

MATT. If it's a risk, it's a risk for both of us. But it could also be a great ride. And I'm in if you are.

TOM. —

MATT. We need more voices like yours, Tom. Like ours. The party is settling in too far to the right.

TOM. Including Jenkins.

MATT. I told you, he's not as right as you think. And he's trying to follow Reagan's example and pick a mix of moderates and conservatives to advise him, but at the moment the balance is with people like Hale and Baker and Chase.

TOM. Baker, that wingnut?

MATT. One of the best things about Steve is that he wants to be challenged – he is not interested in a bunch of sycophants and 'yes' men.

TOM. I wouldn't be any of that.

MATT. No you wouldn't. And if Steve gets you in the mix, there will be real opportunity to effect policy.

TOM. And all you need from me is a little whistling past the First Amendment.

MATT. You admire Jesus. You said so yourself. You should quote the people you admire.

LISA. *(entering)* I think this box will work well. *(to* MATT*)* See, it's got a lid, in case the bird starts the flapping.

TOM. *(looking back at the bird)* He stopped breathing.

LISA. Oh, Tom…

TOM. I guess the impact was too much.

LISA. I'm sorry.

> (**LISA** *places her hand on the bird and closes her eyes for a moment.*)

TOM. What are you doing?

LISA. I'm, saying a prayer.

TOM. Why – do birds have souls?

LISA. I don't know.

TOM. You don't know?

LISA. No.

TOM. I thought the Bible said that animals don't have souls.

LISA. It doesn't say that directly, but –

TOM. I thought it did.

LISA. The inference is, from Genesis, that when –

TOM. I thought it was a biblical *fact.*

LISA. *(to* **TOM***)* What are you doing?

TOM. Nothing.

(**MATT** *is checking his cell.*)

LISA. You sound so angry, suddenly.

TOM. I'm just thinking about, souls.

LISA. But it sounds like you're, blaming me for something.

TOM. No, I was just wondering why your God, in his almighty wisdom, would have denied animals their souls.

LISA. *My* God?

(**TOM** *places the bird in the box.*)

TOM. Matt – tell me again the timing on this decision? Matt – ?

MATT. Hold on.

(As **MATT** *is focused on his cell,* **LISA** *exits with the shoebox.*)

(At the cell, looking at a message. Under his breath.) Fuck – fuck – fuck.

TOM. Matt?

MATT. *(distracted)* What. *(paying attention now, as* **TOM** *is staring at him)* Sorry, what?

TOM. You said we have through tomorrow?

MATT. You can have until tomorrow afternoon. But here's a new wrinkle. This latest email is saying that they're pushing Steve to vet David Wilcox as well.

TOM. For Vice President?

MATT. I thought we had buried that possibility but fucking Baker wants to throw him back into the mix. The Governor's very comfortable with Wilcox, they did a lot of work on tax reform together.

TOM. He'll never win with Wilcox. Never.

(**LISA** *enters.*)

MATT. No, he won't. And that's what I keep telling him. But it may have been a mistake for me to come here.

TOM. Mistake?

MATT. Strategically, I mean. If I'd just called, instead of traveled, I'd be with Steve now and able to pre-empt any of Baker's latest stupidity. But. I thought it was important, that I see you both in person. It was important and I – it was something I just really wanted to do. So. Tom, I keep telling you that we need you. You are the guy – not just in comparison to a wingnut like Wilcox – you are the model candidate.

LISA. Except for the way in which he's not.

MATT. Right. But. I'm a pragmatist. And the way I look at it – Lisa, you said it yourself: people assume things. Tom is not a suspect. He is a white, heterosexual, former military –

TOM. Handsome.

MATT. Kind of handsome southern Senator. *(to* **TOM***)* You are not a suspect. So I think we should focus our –

*(***MATT***'s phone buzzes.)*

(to **TOM** *and* **LISA***)* Sorry. Excuse me. *(He turns away slightly.)* Hi, yes. Put him on. Yes, Governor.

LISA. *(to* **TOM***)* No!

TOM. What, no?

LISA. No, no, no. He's not supposed to be calling now! Not yet!

MATT. *(into phone)* I sent a detailed email to John about that.

LISA. *(overlapping)* We're supposed to be able to think about this in peace without him calling and pressuring you, Tom! For a few hours at least!

TOM. What do you want me to do about it?

MATT. *(into phone)* Tell them we can't print twenty-five billion dollars every time they want to fund a new program.

LISA. This is ridiculous. And on our anniversary besides, my God!

MATT. *(into phone)* Sure thing. I'll follow up on that tomorrow. Okay, hold on.

LISA *(overlapping, to* **TOM***)* Tell him we've barely started discussing it yet, and he can just wait. It's disrespectful.

(**MATT** *hands over the phone and* **TOM** *reaches for it.)*

MATT. *(to* **LISA***)* It's for you.

LISA. What?

MATT. The Governor would like to speak to you.

LISA. Me?

MATT. Yes.

(**MATT** *continues holding out his phone to* **LISA***, who is just staring at it)*

MATT. Would you like to speak to him, or should I...?

LISA. Sure, of course. Of course. (**LISA** *takes the phone.)* Hello? Hi, yes, of course I do, Governor, how are you? Thank you. That's right, twenty years. Oh, well, we first met at a concert. I'd rather not say.

TOM. Don't say.

LISA. Barry Manilow. Yes, that is embarrassing.

MATT. *(to* **TOM***)* We can do damage control later.

LISA. The shelter, you know about the shelter? Thank you, but it's not me, it's the women who deserve all the praise. Most of them come from such difficult backgrounds, and some of their stories, it just breaks your heart. I would like that very much, thank you, I would be happy to show you around. Okay, I will. Did you need to speak to – okay. Yes, good talking with you too. I will. Bye.

(**LISA** *hangs up the phone. Beat.)*

(to **MATT***)* No, no, no, no, no.

MATT. What?

LISA. You told him about the shelter?

MATT. Yes.

LISA. And he thinks he can just call me and get on my good side and then wham-bam thank you Ma'am, the deal is done?

TOM. Wham-bam thank you Ma'am?

MATT. He wants you on his side, what is so terrible about that?

LISA. He's trying to use the shelter, he's trying to use the women to get to me.

TOM. *(gently)* You want people to know about the shelter. You want people to help.

LISA. But he's trying to play me.

MATT. Lisa, why do you keep – yes, it's a measure of how much he wants you and Tom, that when he heard about the shelter he saw it as a way to support something that you both believe in. But if the great passion of your life were, say, the local Azalea Society, he wouldn't bother, believe me.

LISA. —

MATT. Steve respects what you're doing there because what you're doing there is important. It's changing lives. Lives like Tanya's.

TOM. And there are so many like Tanya.

LISA. We had three new girls come in just yesterday, we barely have room for them all.

He said that when he comes to Richmond again, he'd like to see firsthand what we're doing. When is he coming to Richmond?

MATT. He's giving a speech at the Coliseum in early September.

LISA. If Jenkins came to our shelter, if he stopped with us for five minutes, we could probably raise…tens of thousands of dollars.

TOM. Hundreds of thousands.

MATT. And if he mentioned it in a speech, a lot more than that.

LISA. Do you think he'd really stop by?

MATT. I know he'd really stop by. And he'd bring a parade of photographers with him.

(**LISA** *looks at* **TOM**)

For almost twenty-five years I have given up all pretence at a normal life. But this is why. For a moment like this. I agreed with Jay all those years ago, Tom. And this is your time. We will figure out the language and I think you're right, privacy is the key. Jack Kemp didn't like talking about his faith for the same reason.

TOM. Jack Kemp was devout.

MATT. Yes, but he was adamant that it be private. And it should be private, I agree with you. It's just that in this three-month period that might be a little tricky. Might. It might not. And once you're elected there will be many more important things to worry about. Meanwhile, I think we can engineer the 'question', and I think we should. So that when you talk about God and faith – you talk about the Founders and the First, and at the same time you give just enough of a bone, just enough of a signal that you're 'one of us' (*at* **LISA**'*s face*) without – without betraying your morals. And then I think we can move on to other things. Because there are so many other things.

LISA. What makes you think you can control the circumstances in which/ he will be –

MATT. Lisa, forget the campaigning for a moment. Forget the distractions and the inevitable bullshit. Is there anyone that you can think of who would be a better leader for this country than Tom? Anyone with his vision, with his integrity, with his capability; anyone at *all*...?

LISA. ...No.

MATT. They call it public service for a reason.

(**LISA** *nods.*)

TOM. ...I should be clear – I would want an active role in a Jenkins administration.

MATT. Absolutely.

TOM. The vice presidency has been, historically, the land where politicians go to die.

MATT. It's changed, Tom, you know that.

TOM. I realize it has changed, but Steve strikes me as someone who wouldn't mind changing it back and I'm not going to leave the Senate to be Mr. Step-n-Fetchit for the Jenkins administration.

MATT. I told you, he wants real participation.

TOM. As long as we're clear.

MATT. We're clear. I can't wait to get the two of you in a room together.

TOM. —

MATT. Worst case – if we lose, you're still the very much admired junior Senator from Virginia. But if we win, you're at the front of the line.

TOM. Matt, your confidence is infectious.

MATT. I get it from you. I do. The prospect of you as Vice President, and then you in the White House, it's exhilarating. Isn't it?

TOM. Yes. It is.

MATT. So. I'd like to set up a call between you and Steve tomorrow morning. And then if all parties are agreed, we'd like to set up a dinner meeting for tomorrow night. You and Lisa, Steve, Pam, Charles, Eric, myself. We'll go to Georgetown – Amanda Wright has offered her townhouse for the meeting. That way we won't be seen.

LISA. I've always wanted to see Amanda Wright's famous townhouse. She has a world class art collection. She has a Rembrandt, the lady has a Rembrandt.

MATT. *(looking at his cell, to* **TOM***)* How is 9 a.m. for you? For the phone call with Steve?

TOM. Can we make it noon? Lisa asked me to go to church with her tomorrow.

LISA. Go to church with me?

MATT. *(to* **TOM***)* So let's make it eight with Steve, how's that?

TOM. Eight should be fine.

MATT. *(looking at his cell again)* Okay. And Lisa, it's September 9, that Steve will be speaking in Richmond. Can we set up a visit at the shelter around say, three o'clock? Lisa?

LISA. ...You're good. You're both good. All of you, I'll give you that. The Governor too.

MATT. What?

LISA. How is it, that you knew we would be here today, Matt?

MATT. You always spend your anniversary at home.

LISA. Maybe we wanted to do something different this year.

MATT. Every year for the last twenty, you have spent your anniversary at home. You have grilled steak on the barbeque. You have discovered an astounding new Burgundy. And you have had cake.

LISA. But maybe, with Jay gone, we wanted to find new traditions. Didn't you consider that possibility?

MATT. No.

LISA. Our anniversary has always been shared with Jay, and, until a year ago, with you too. So I would think that you would have had to consider the possibility that we may have wanted to do things differently this year. I mean, you couldn't fly to Richmond only to find out we were in the Bahamas.

TOM. My office told him.

LISA. —

TOM. My office confirmed that we were here.

LISA. Then somebody in your office should be fired.

TOM. They checked with me.

LISA. You knew?

TOM. I thought Matt wanted something – not *this* – not us on the ticket. But something. I thought that he probably had campaign business in Richmond and that he wanted to use the opportunity while he/ was here –

LISA. So you allowed him to come here without asking me.

TOM. I knew you'd say no.

LISA. That's not an acceptable answer.

TOM. I knew you'd say no, and I wanted to see him. He's the man my brother loved best in the world, he's our dear friend, he makes me laugh – and Lisa, I've needed to laugh. I wanted to see him. And I knew you would too, once he was here. And I was right.

LISA. Do you have a sudden urge to know God, Tom?

TOM. You asked me to go to church with you.

LISA. No, Tom. I practically begged you to go to church with me. And you said no.

(to **MATT***)*

I didn't realize until now how much you need me, Matt. I mean, I obviously knew you'd need me to look nice and wave and maybe give a little speech here or there. But you *need* me.

MATT. Lisa, I'm not saying this to be rude. But it's Tom we need.

LISA. There is not a bumpkin left in Appalachia who would believe that statement. You don't just need Tom, you need everything that comes with Tom. You need my impeccable Christian credentials. You need my faith.

MATT. We don't need your faith.

LISA. You want Tom to lie. There's no way around it, you want him to lie about God. You are not going to be able to 'engineer' the 'question'. You can't count on that kind of control of the media or of anyone else.

MATT. I'm not claiming control of the media, I'm just saying that after the campaign we/ will have different –

LISA. What do you mean, after the campaign? There is no such thing. This country is all campaign, all the time. They're already taking polls on the next one.

TOM. That's a little over the top, isn't it?

LISA. You want him to go to church – with me – and lie.

MATT. You know, Lisa, my Dad, he goes to services almost every week. He likes the people. He likes the community. He likes the music and the oratory. I'm honestly not sure how he feels about God. He never says. I've sometimes wondered whether he believes or not. And if not, is he lying? By going to church? Do you really want to be the God police? We can work around this.

LISA. You've been here barely two hours and already you're trying to spin me!

MATT. I'm not trying to spin you.

LISA. Really? Do you even know the difference anymore? *(to* TOM*)* It's a betrayal. To lie about God is a betrayal.

MATT. You can't betray a God that you don't believe in.

LISA. He can betray a wife! *(to* TOM*)* How would I sit across the breakfast table from you, knowing you would lie about something so basic? How would you look our daughter in the eye if you did that?

TOM. You know how I will look my daughter in the eye? By keeping this country from going bankrupt on her. By working to protect her future. By bringing the climate back in to the discussion. And I am uniquely qualified to do that. Me. Me.

LISA. Wow.

MATT. Both you and Tom will be able to have such a positive impact, but we need to pick our battles.

LISA. I'm sorry you were born gay, Matt.

TOM. Lisa, get a hold of yourself.

LISA. I am. And Jay was sorry for you too – no, not sorry. Sad. As much as you broke his heart, he was sad for you. Because you had to get so used to lying. But I'm not used to that – and I don't want to get used to that.

MATT. Lisa, how does anyone actually live in your little black and white world?!

LISA. That is not/ fair –

MATT. Because Tom is not a black and white candidate – that's what makes him special. But it also make him vulnerable. You said to me earlier that Tom needs a friend right now –

LISA. Yes – and instead, you come here/ and –

MATT. But doesn't he need you most of all? You keep talking about your faith, your faith, your faith – but what I keep wondering is: Where is your faith in Tom?! I have it. Jay certainly had it – Jay thought his big brother hung the moon.

LISA. Jay also kept him grounded – and that's what I do too. We are his foundation. Maybe/ you don't think you need that with your busy important life, but we are the ones –

MATT. *(overlapping)* So you really think Jay would admire you standing in the way of this opportunity for Tom? Do you really/ think –

TOM. Would you please stop using my brother! Both of you! Jay this, Jay that – he's not here! He will never be here!

LISA. Tom.

TOM. Lisa, I love you, I love you more than my own life. But I agree with Matt, how can I betray a God I don't believe in? And I stopped believing in God when Jay –

LISA. Don't say it.

TOM. I think the universe follows certain laws, most of which I don't pretend to understand. But life as we live it, I think life is random, and we do the best we can while we're here. Hopefully we don't blow each other up, or crush each other's spirit, or find ourselves hurtling into the path of an oncoming truck before our time.

LISA. Tom –

TOM. Before his time.

LISA. —

TOM. So we do the best we can. And as Americans, through a combination of bravery and foresight and, and unbelievable, gall – we have this magnificent country – this *astonishing* country. Never another like it in the history of the world. Never. We are the shining city on the hill, and not because of a God, but because of us – *us!* And we can't be shy about what makes us special. Lisa, I have gifts, and I intend to use them. We are at a crucial time in our history and we can't afford to be precious about the small stuff.

LISA. The small stuff?

TOM. Yes. I'm sorry, but yes.

LISA. *(beat)* So this is how it starts. I've always wondered.

TOM. I only mean – everything in its place.

LISA. Yes, that's very clear, thank you. So. You boys need to do your thing here. Let me know what you decide.

(She moves to leave and then goes back to **TOM.** *)*

I've always believed that if I really needed you, that when it really mattered, you'd be there for me. No matter what. And me for you. Because I do have faith in you. So if you decide to go forward with this, I will support you, I will stand by your side.

But if you lie, just once, if you actively affirm a faith that you don't have – please don't do it, Tommy, please. Because you'd be asking me to be complicit and I can't do that. So I'd have to leave.

TOM. Lisa, we've never made ultimatums with each other –

LISA. *(taking in both* **TOM** *and* **MATT***)* Then can you tell me? How to do that? Because I'd really like to know.

TOM. —

LISA. God is real, Tom. And while you may not accept that, you know it is at the very core of who I am. And if you lie about Him, I think something would break in me, and I don't think you could ever fix that.

(**LISA** *looks at them both, then exits.*)

(*silence*)

MATT. You should go to her.

(**TOM** *walks over to the window and looks out at the garden.*)

Do you think she's serious? About leaving?

TOM. I don't know. She's gotten more serious since Jay died. We both have.

MATT. You should go to her.

TOM. I heard you the first time.

(*beat*)

MATT. Jay wanted to get married, I guess you knew that.

TOM. Yes.

MATT. Did you also know that we had a huge fight about it? How could I marry him and still work for Jenkins? This was the big time for me. A presidential candidate – I mean, come *on* – it's what I've always wanted!

(*He's got* **TOM**'s *attention.*)

We sweat blood to gain traction in this insane, ass-kicking business, don't we?

TOM. —

MATT. And I love it – and I have worked all my life to get here. All my life.

TOM. What are you getting at?

MATT. When Steve hired me, he said, "I understand you're a homosexual, but we're all sinners and you're the smartest sinner in the room."

(*at* **TOM**'s *expression*)

I like Steve. And I think he's sincerely fond of me. I'm pretty sure he prays for me.

He's even said that he thinks of me like a son.

MATT. But.

If I could do it all over again, I would say yes. To Jay. I would say yes.

I don't have that option.

Tom – if you're in, I'm going to set that up. But you need to talk to Lisa first. And I need to get on the road.

TOM. No, don't leave yet. We'll have dinner, we'll figure this out – all of us together –

Lisa will come around.

MATT. Why don't you call me when you've had a chance to sleep on everything.

TOM. I don't need to sleep on it.

MATT. Listen to me! This is your time. And it might not come again. But I want you to sleep on it before you decide. And whatever you do – don't lose Lisa. Please don't lose her.

(Lights shift.)

(A week or so later. **TOM** *is at his first press avail after the press announcement for Vice President. He has just finished answering a question.* **LISA** *is there.)*

TOM. And that's why our plan holds the best way forward and it's why I am so proud to be a part of this ticket. All right, they're telling me we've got time for one more question. But before that, I'd just like to say that it means so much to Lisa and me, that Steve wanted to make this announcement in our hometown. The pundits keep describing Virginia as a battleground state. Well, not this year, folks. Okay, last question. Yes, the gentleman at the back.

REPORTER (VOICE). Senator, your opponent has gotten some heat from the Christian Right for being hostile to matters of faith. Do you agree with his use of the First Amendment in answering his critics?

TOM. I haven't heard all the details yet – but speaking generally, yes, it's a private matter and it's important that we respect his privacy on this. I do find it interesting that he can be so eloquent on the subject of the First Amendment, yet barely on speaking terms with the Second.

REPORTER (VOICE). But Senator, Governor Jenkins is very vocal about his faith – are you saying you're more in line with your opponent than with your running mate?

TOM. *(smiling)* No honeymoon for the new guy, huh? I've only been at this, what, twenty-five minutes and you're looking to stir up controversy already? And this from my hometown paper. But to answer your question, the Governor and I have different personalities, so we express ourselves differently and – but yes, simply put, I feel fortunate in having a faith that has been a centering part of my – our family has had a pretty tough year and the Bible says – I think it's Proverbs – that when…

(A long beat. Embarrassingly long.)

Here's the thing. We had an official religion. Right here in Virginia until 1786. How would you all like to be Episcopalians? Not that I have anything against Episcopalians, but I don't think we want that. So if you want to know about my faith, look around you. Because my faith rests in you. And in this country, and in myself. But most of all, it lies in the woman I had the good sense to marry twenty years ago: Lisa Christine Trevor. All you really need to know about my faith is to look at her.

As for the rest, all due respect –

I am not willing to stand in front of America and politicize God.

(Lights out.)

End of Play.

www.ingramcontent.com/pod-product-compliance
Lightning Source LLC
Chambersburg PA
CBHW072152130726
47909CB00004BB/1652